STAR WARS®

EPISODE I

I Am a Jedi

by Qui-Gon Jinn

as told to Marc Cerasini
Insides designed by Iain Morris

A Scholastic *Star Wars*® Storybook

▲SCHOLASTIC

www.starwars.com

ISBN: 0 439 01245 7
Printed in Italy
3 5 7 9 10 8 6 4

My name is Qui-Gon Jinn.

I am a Jedi.

The Jedi are a very special group of beings.

For many thousands of years, we have worked to promote **peace** and **justice** in the universe.

Jedi Training

Jedi training is very hard
and begins at an early age.

Young Jedi
are raised by

Jedi Masters

and taught
the Jedi ways.

Jedi Padawan: Obi-Wan Kenobi

A Jedi student is called an apprentice or **Padawan.**

Jedi Masters train their Padawans to be Jedi Knights. My Padawan is a young Jedi named

Obi-Wan Kenobi.

He began his training with me when he was a young boy.

The Lightsaber

The lightsaber is the weapon of the Jedi.

Each Jedi must build his own lightsaber as part of his training.

Notice the difference between my lightsaber blade and Obi-Wan's.

This is how a lightsaber works.

The **lightsaber handle** holds a power cell that creates energy.

When the lightsaber is turned on, this energy shoots through a crystal and forms an arc of light that can cut through anything—except another lightsaber blade.

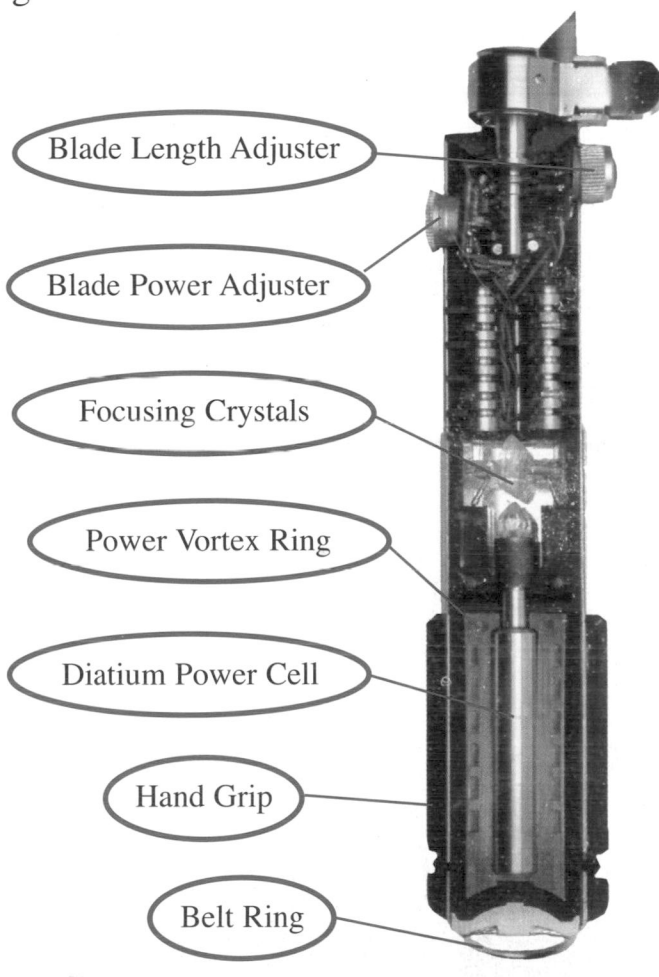

Blade Length Adjuster

Blade Power Adjuster

Focusing Crystals

Power Vortex Ring

Diatium Power Cell

Hand Grip

Belt Ring

The Jedi Temple

The Jedi Temple is the center of Jedi **teaching** and **training.**

The Jedi Temple is found in the heart of the city-planet Coruscant.

Ki-Adi-Mundi

Saesee Tinn

Even Piell

Yaddle

Oppo Rancisis

Yarael Poof

Adi Gallia

At the top of the Jedi Temple sits this very important room. It is the place where the Jedi Council meets.

The Jedi Council

The Jedi are ruled by the Jedi Council. The Council is made up of very wise Jedi.

Members of the Jedi Council come from many worlds.

Plo Koon

Yoda

Mace Windu

Not all humans can be Jedi, and not all Jedi are human.

Depa Billaba

Eeth Koth

Master Yoda

A very important member of the Jedi Council is Master Yoda.

Yoda may be small, but do not be fooled.

Size matters not.

Yoda is one of the most powerful living Jedi.

Master Windu

Mace Windu is another important Jedi. He sits on the Jedi Council with Yoda. Together, they help the Council make many important decisions.

One of the Council's tasks is to test newcomers and rule whether or not they should be trained as Jedi.

Anakin Skywalker is one such newcomer...

Anakin Skywalker

I met Anakin Skywalker on the desert planet Tatooine.

At the age of nine, Anakin was already too old to begin the Jedi training. But he was a very special child.

Anakin raced Pods.

Podracing is very difficult for humans.

It demands **Jedi-like** reflexes.

Jedi Testing

I brought Anakin before the Jedi Council.

The Council tested Anakin.

They ruled that he did have Jedi reflexes.

He was strong in the Force.

The Force

The Force is a mysterious form of energy that connects all living things. We Jedi learn to be sensitive to the Force. It is a source of great strength.

But a true Jedi uses the Force only for knowledge and defence,

never for **attack**.

While a Jedi Knight may be a great warrior,

it is **not war** that makes a Jedi great.

A Jedi's greatness
comes from his wise
mastery of the Force.

The Force is strong
and can be used to
do many things.

A Jedi can move
objects with the Force.

He can protect others
and
battle evil.

Young Jedi are taught to
use the Force for **good**;

to seek **wisdom** not power.

But there is danger.

The Force has two sides:
a **light side** and a

dark side.

The Light Side and The Dark Side

All Jedi must beware of the dark side.

It lives on fear and hatred

and can only lead to evil.

Darth Sidious, Lord of the Sith

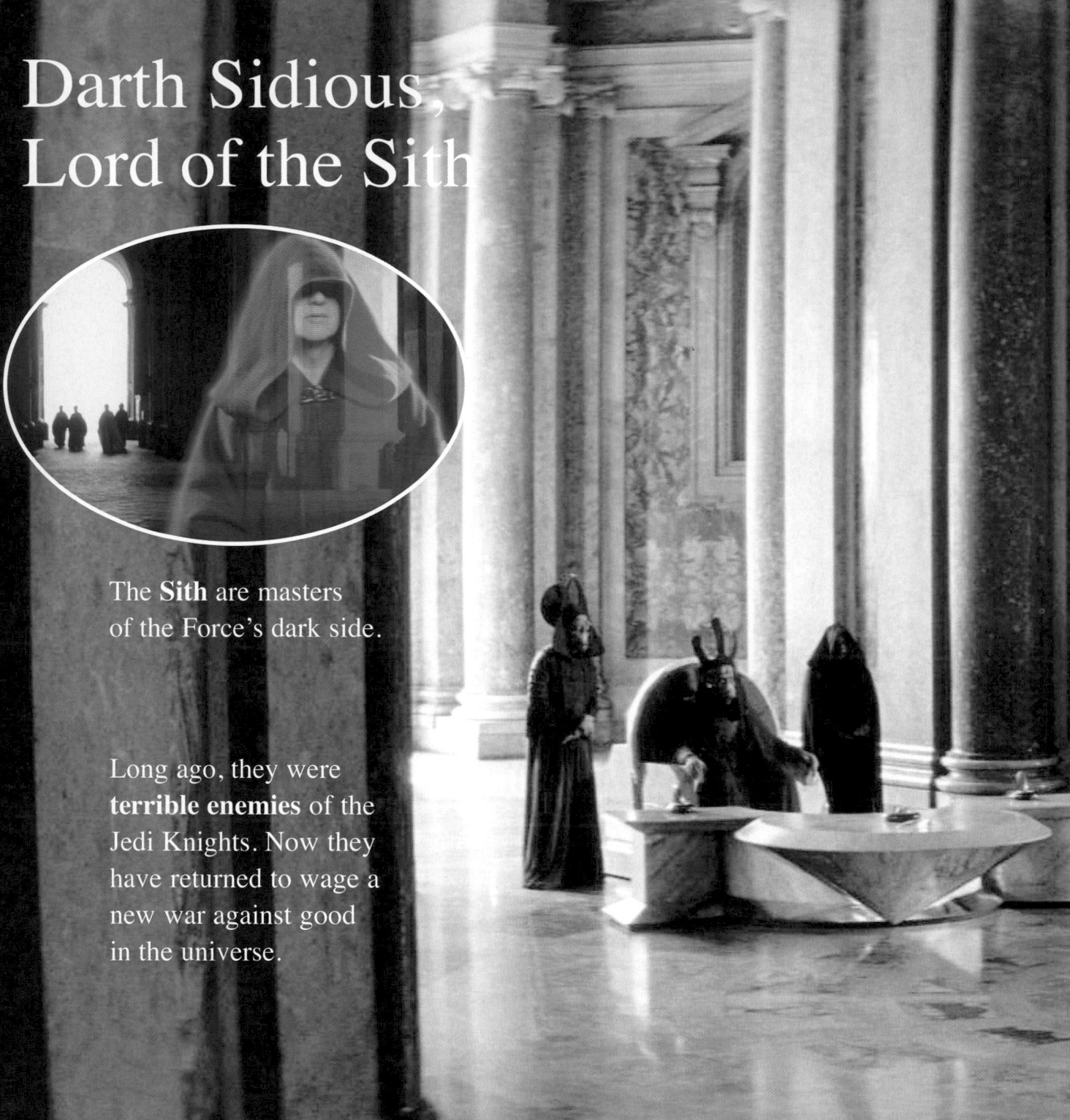

The **Sith** are masters of the Force's dark side.

Long ago, they were **terrible enemies** of the Jedi Knights. Now they have returned to wage a new war against good in the universe.

Darth Sidious is the new Sith Lord.

With his power, he uses others to do his **evil bidding.**

The Neimoidians and their army of Trade Federation battle droids are simply puppets under his **dark control.**

Darth Maul, Sith Apprentice

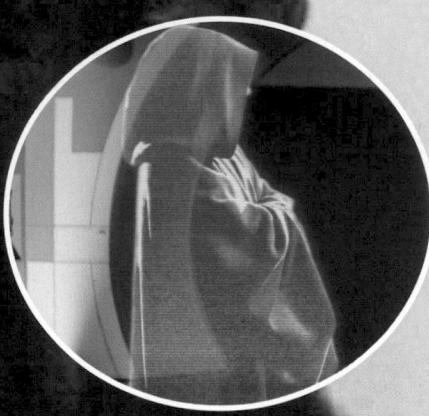

Darth Sidious is teaching the ways of the dark side to an apprentice.

His name is **Darth Maul.**

Darth Maul uses a special lightsaber.

It has two blades, which makes it **twice** as **deadly**.

Battle

Darth Maul and Darth Sidious are fierce enemies of all Jedi Knights.

I battled Darth Maul on the planet Tatooine.

I battled Maul again on the planet Naboo. Obi-Wan Kenobi, my apprentice, joined me in that battle.

I am Obi-Wan Kenobi. I defeated Darth Maul and became a Jedi Knight.

Now it is my turn to take an apprentice. My Padawan is Anakin Skywalker.

If Anakin **works hard** to learn the Jedi ways,

he will become a **Jedi Knight**, too.

The Jedi Ways

Like me, Qui-Gon, Yoda and a thousand generations of young Padawans before him,

The Jedi Code

Jedi are the guardians of peace in the galaxy.
Jedi use their powers to defend and protect, never to attack others.
Jedi respect all life, in any form.
Jedi serve others rather than rule over them, for the good of the galaxy.
Jedi seek to improve themselves through knowledge and training.

Anakin Skywalker will soon learn the ways of the most

respected and **powerful**

force for **good** in the universe...

the Jedi.